Peaceful pictures create peaceful thoughts

HEATHER LAVINE

THESE ARE THE
MOMENTS

A Collection of Short Stories

The stories in this book are a work of fiction. All characters, places and incidents are from the Authors imagination or are used fictionally. Any resemblance to an actual event or person, living or dead, is entirely coincidental.

Published under SJK Publishing authority; November 2009, Ellijay Georgia.

ISBN # 1449904068

Copyright 2009 © by Heather LaVine

www.heatherlavine.com

All rights reserved

This collection of short stories is dedicated to my children; Sebastien, Jade and Katlin. Thank you for bringing the joy of a day to my life.

Dear Reader:

This book is a collection of short stories for your reading enjoyment. Some are new, written this year. Some are old, written as far back as the year 2000; all are being published for the first time in this book. I hope you enjoy reading them as much as I enjoyed writing them.

Always Yours,

Heather LaVine

Contents

These are the Moments

Tis the Season

"Just" Friends

Falling Apart

Secret Family

It's Who I Am

Waiting On Flight 7768

It Wasn't Murder

A Bear Saves The Day

These are the Moments

*Includes excerpts of "I Could Not Ask For More" – Sara Evans

She sits down in a patch of sunlight that is streaming through the window onto the pewter carpet, dodging the sheer burgundy curtains that are being carried by the wind.

The sky is a shade of blue so startling that she finds herself staring at it as if she's never before been beneath its cover, and she thinks of blue gumballs and Easter eggs and a smile creeps across her lips before she can stop it.

Outside, the sky exhales, punctuated by the wind chimes hanging on her neighbor's balcony. She loves the sound of wind chimes. They always seem melancholic and wistful, even on days when the sun is as garish as it is now.

A yellow cat sighs happily over on the bed in the corner, and another -- a big, jiggly creature in black and white whose sheer size contradicts a feline's reputation for grace -- comes galloping into the room, his eyes dilated and wild with the fresh air.

He looks at her for a moment, considers, and then abandons his original mission and strolls over, a locomotive inside him, bull-dozing her arms and legs with his head in a bid for love. She complies without further prodding.

 Music plays, only her favorite songs, tunes that slip beneath her folded legs and lift her so high that she can no longer see all the things that have been making her so unhappy these days. They seem to get smaller and smaller as she rises higher, feeling, for the first time in too long, like she has been reunited with her spirit.

If only she could capture this moment and use it as a salve for all her wounds. Instead, she closes her eyes and lets her lids warm in the sun.

The song throbs along with her pulse and its words fall onto her lap, like a gift from some invisible friend: *These are the moments I thank God that I'm alive; these are the moments I'll remember all my life.... These are the moments I know Heaven must exist; these are the moments I know all I need is this.*

She mimics the yellow cat and sighs deeply.

"JUST" FRIENDS

Jada Brown was giddy as usual. Playing a game of adult tag with her friends the sun shone brightly on their youthful twenty-something bodies.

They were seven in number, but Jada only really knew four out of the bunch. Being in New York City for only six months, she had met her new 'associates' as she liked to call them, through her job as a bartender.

Within moments the game broke out into a free for all, with everybody chasing the petite Casey around the picnic table that was cluttered with the remains of their earlier lunch.

"You're it." Jada said into Casey's red ear as she leaped on top of her immediately causing a cascade of bodies to fall into the old ritual of a pig pile.

"OK! OK!" Casey's small voice screamed. "Shit, I can't breathe down here!"

"What! We can't hear you!" Peter yelled, his short blond hair shining brightly in the afternoon sun, grinning down at Casey from somewhere up high.

"Get off!" Jada commanded, afraid that the fragile Casey might be seriously hurt.

Immediately, she felt the weight on her back ease up, as one by one, the gang began to break up and back away. When Jada finally crawled away from Casey and stood on her own two feet, the sight of Casey laying so frightfully still on her stomach filled her own stomach with panic juice.

With the exception of the rumbling of the passing cars, and the other gregarious adults and children playing nearby on this Friday afternoon, everything else was quiet. No one in the circle of six that was gathered around the crushed-looking Casey seemed to even breathe. Including the fallen seventh member, whose short blond hair was a muddy mess, and who's once gleaming white polo shirt was pushed way up exposing her back, which was tattooed with red blotches from their violent skirmish.

"Casey?" questioned Jimmy.

"Casey?!" Brittany repeated a little more urgently.

Finally, not knowing what else to do, Jada rushed forward to turn the deflated Casey over, but something stopped her in her tracks.

Casey was moving.

Slowly, she pushed herself up-but only slightly, then, like an inexperienced beetle, flipped herself over on her back.

Her face was blood red, flat looking and deflated like the rest of her skinny body, but the smile on her face was fat like an overweight pimp and filled with delicious secret amusement.

Like a robot she lifted up a stiff right arm, and flung a long middle finger into the air. "You assholes!" She screeched, "You could have killed me!" Then she broke up into dry laughter; coughing too, as the rest of the group let out thankful sighs and laughed out of sheer relief.

"Damn Casey," Peter said, helping Jimmy get Casey back on her feet, "we thought we killed you!"

"We sure did," Nicole added.

"And what the hell were you people gonna to do with me?" Casey asked, still laughing and staggering over to the cooler for a beer.

"I would have opted to throw your ass in the pond!" Brittany blurted out, showing her pearly whites as she laughed.

Tired and relieved, Jada took a few sips from her thermos...suddenly she had an idea, "Don't move you guys!" Having said that, she rushed back to her bag a little farther down to grab her camera.

"No more pictures!" She heard Nicole scream behind her. "I look terrible." Everybody laughed, even though they all knew, like Jada knew, that Nikki was dead serious.

Ignoring her, Jada dove into her bag. A few seconds later, a puzzled look spread across her face. She searched again, "What the..." she said out loud, "where the hell...hey who took my camera?!" Grabbing the whole bag, she stalked over to where the others sat. All looked as confused as she did.

"You can't find it?" Brenda asked, a beer in hand.

"Good." Nikki added offhandedly.

"Like you all don't know that already. Stop playing around, who took it?" Jada questioned. They all only smiled and shook their sweaty faces.

"Seriously J, none of us took it." Jimmy finally said. Jimmy wasn't a practical joker; if he said no one had it...that probably meant no one did.

Unless of course the guilty party hadn't let him in on the joke, which they probably wouldn't since Jimmy wasn't a good liar. Frustrated, Jada went back to the spot where they had been playing and searched the area. No camera.

"Is your wallet still there?" Brittany asked from somewhere behind her.

"Yeah, it's here...I just don't understand." Jada turned around to see if anybody was secretly laughing, no one was. "I could have sworn, I put it in the freaking bag!"

Casey chuckled and took a gulp of her beer. "Why would someone steal a cheap disposable camera, yet not take any money?"

Jada was livid. She had taken some damn good pictures with that cheap camera, now some jerk had stolen it right from under their noses. She huffed and puffed as she searched, then finally...seeing the disinterest in everybody else's eyes said, "The hell with it..it's just a camera, I'm calling it a day...."

Later, Jada, Jimmy, Brittany and Casey sat in Jada's hot, small, living room playing an even hotter game of spades. There was a slight dizziness in Jada's head; she wasn't quite feeling herself. Too much time in the sun, maybe?

Across the table she eyed her partner and ex-boyfriend secretly. Every now and then, his dark eyes would drift towards hers and she would look away. He had come in late one night at 'The Lounge,' looking rather depressed, disheveled and out of place. Always attracted to the 'preppie' type, Jada had spotted him immediately and slyly made her way over to his end of the bar to serve him.

Three hours and a lot of coke with rums later, she knew practically everything about him. Everything, except for why he had came in looking the way he did. He 'didn't want to talk about that.' So she had never mentioned it again, after all she was a total stranger.

They were 'friends' at first, and then started seriously dating a very short while after that. Four months later, he was always so 'busy' that she could never get in touch with him. In the end, they decided it would be better if they just remained 'friends'.

Yeah, friends who slept together every now and then, she thought to herself. He looked up at her, their eye's met, and as usual he seemed to know what she was thinking. He smiled at her, a dark mysterious smile, as dark as his huge liquid, brown eyes. She smiled back slyly and threw a spade out on the table.

Brittany threw her an evil look; Casey only smiled, obviously plotting her next move. Jada looked back at Jimmy... oh yes, he would be spending the night.

Brittany and Casey left around 11:00 after Jimmy and Jada had whopped them at Spades. Brenda had given Jada a hug on her way out the door and had told her to 'have fun.' Apparently their friends knew about her and Jimmy.

Early the next morning, around 2 a.m., Jimmy kissed her gently on the cheek and promised to call later. She rolled over, happy with their little arrangement, and went back to sleep.

Three apartments down, Mr. Ligget heard a door open and close. He crept over to his own door, and with the chain still latched on, ignorantly opened it. The tall, dark, well-built man was leaving once again in the middle of the night. He turned to look at Mr.Ligget who fearlessly stared back at him with old yellow eyes that had seen plenty. The young man smiled at Mr.Ligget.

Mr.Ligget slammed the door and locked all locks.

Creepy old man, thought Jimmy as he walked towards the elevators, content with his life as it was.

TIS' THE SEASON

She called and woke me up, sounding scared. I tried telling her it would be okay, that this type of thing was normal, especially this time of the year.

She insisted that I do what she asked. I think it was something about a closet. I'm not sure, I was still half asleep. So I told her okay, whatever you want, just to make her happy. I wish I had listened to her. Instead I went back to bed. These days I don't get around much without help and I listen to advice instead of thinking that I'm always right.

Dark clouds gathered overhead, causing the early afternoon to look more like dusk. Parking lots all throughout the metroplex were almost empty, everyone jamming up the interstates in a rush to get home.

Radio stations that normally played music all day were now sending only emergency broadcasts across their airwaves. Everything had a chaotic feeling to it, from the sky to the roads.

"Massive storms are streaking across the State today," the newscaster was saying, "stay tuned for our storm expert, Tom Lander, coming up after the break."

"I'm going out for a cigarette Mom," Sara said walking away from the television set.

"Hold on, I'm coming with you," her mom replied, walking behind her. "Let's make it quick though, I want to hear the rest of the broadcast."

Once outside, Sara glanced up at the sky and noticed how fast the dark clouds were moving. "I think we're in for a doozie, Mom," she said.

"Maybe," her mom said. "If we hear the siren then we know that we're in trouble."

"Siren?" Sara questioned, "What siren?"

"If a tornado is spotted within five miles of here, a town alarm will go off. And trust me, you can't miss it." Her mom replied. "The first time I heard it, I thought I was going to have a heart attack it was so loud!"

"If there's one thing I hate about Texas, it's the storms," Sara said. "At least in

Vermont all we have to worry about are blizzards."

"Shh," her mom said with her ear pressed to the screen of her window, listening to the weather report that had just come back on.

Sara caught one word as she walked past the front door, which was also open. "Ike."

"Did they say Ike?" Sara questioned as she dropped her cigarette and raced inside to stand in front of the TV.

As she saw the area where she lived on the screen she said, "Oh my gosh Mom, I need the phone." Her mom pointed to it on the table and Sara began frantically dialing her house. "Matt's asleep," she explained, her heart feeling heavy, "Mom, my house is only two miles from Ike!"

"There's a tornado in Ike. Get in the closet. Or better yet, go over to Brian's house. At least his house is brick." Sara said without greeting when her boyfriend finally answered the phone. "Please Matt; don't argue with me, it's in Ike right now."

When Sara thought that she had finally convinced Matt, she hung up the phone and walked back outside to look at the sky. "Well, we know we're okay for awhile. It's still an hour away," she said to her mom, who had followed her out and also stood looking at the sky.

"I don't know," her mom replied. "The weather channel just said that there are ten tornadoes between Harris and Kirkland right now. Ike's isn't the only one."

As soon as she finished speaking, the skies turned the blackest that Sara had ever seen and the wind blew so strong that her mother's metal patio set was knocked to its side. Sara could feel the change of tension in the air. "Okay Mom, I think it's time to go inside," Sara said walking back towards the house, her stomach tight with nerves.

Sara and her mom were once again safely inside the house watching the fierce storm brew. The wind was howling an ear-splitting screech, hail bounced off the ground and cars like ping pong balls, tree limbs fell on the roof, thunder shook the house and lightning charged the air with an energy Sara had never felt before.

As they watched, a small section of their neighbor's roof came flying off and landed on top of Brenda's flower garden. "Should we get in the closet?" Sara asked her mom, not taking her eyes off the menacing sky through the window.

"Yea, I think we better. This is getting bad," she replied, "Grab the weather radio, it's on top of the fridge."

When mother and daughter were settled in the cramped space of the closet, they tuned in the radio. "There are numerous reporting's of tornadoes in the Caper area. If you live in this area, seek shelter immediately," they heard the broadcaster say. "Gusts up to 120 miles per hour and softball size hail should be expected. Again: seek shelter immediately if you're in the Caper area." *beep beeeep beep*

They huddled together with just a flashlight illuminating the dark and listened to the wind tear at their home. They could hear objects being thrown against the side of the house and a window shatter somewhere nearby.

Sara held tightly to her mother's hand, expecting at any moment to be picked up by the wind and tossed aside. Just when Sara thought it was never going to end, all was quiet.

They both sat there for a full minute, listening.

Finally, Sara gingerly pushed open the closet door and stepped out into the bedroom with her mother right behind her. Looking up, they saw the sun shining brightly through what used to be the ceiling. Walking outdoors, they saw two trees had fallen, one on top of a neighbor's car. The Smith's shed across the street was in their backyard and they no longer had a fence around their property.

"Look," Sara said when she found her voice again, "the sun's shining like nothing just happened."

As they walked around the yard, they saw a few neighbors come out of their own hiding places to assess the damage.

"I'll be right back, I'm going to see if the phones are working." Sara said as she walked back inside and came right back out without the phone.

"Listen Mom, I'm sorry to leave you with this mess, but I need to get home. I'm worried about Matt. I'll come back tomorrow, okay? The phone lines are down so I've got to go." And she was off without waiting for a reply, racing home in her truck that had somehow only got a few dents on the hood from the hail.

When Sara arrived in Chens, the town she had moved to just the month before, she saw that several houses had been badly damaged and her stomach went tight for the second time that day. As she turned onto her road she saw her neighbor walking through rubble that had once been his home. She pulled over and jumped out of her truck, running to where her own house was supposed to be.

It looks like a pile of lumber, she thought to herself as she started screaming for Matt, knocking piles of wood over, searching underneath.

"MATT?" Sara ran over to where she thought her closet had once been and started digging through the pile but all she came up with was a handful of soggy clothes.

She frantically searched where their bedroom had been and saw that the bed wasn't even there, it had been blown away by the wind.

Frantically stumbling atop the debris she heard her neighbor call to her from across the street. "Sara. Matt's been taken to the Hospital. They found him about an hour ago," he informed her. "He's alive, but he's seriously injured."

Sara thanked him and rushed off again, not even thinking of her house that was no longer.

Falling Apart

Sean cut the wheel quickly to the left, trying to avoid the cliff he saw looming large and menacing directly in front of him. Beside him his younger sister Christi, with her brown eyes large and luminous, screamed as is her life was about to end. Sean, trying his hardest to ignore her and concentrate solely on steering the sleek green Mustang that he had just received for his eighteenth birthday, slammed on his brakes and remembered a fraction of a second to late that that was the last thing you were supposed to do while in a skid. His last coherent thought was: *so much for Drivers Ed.*

"Christi? Christi? CHRISTI?" Sean squirmed on the short narrow bed as he screamed his ten year old sisters name over and over again.

Marlene, the night nurse who had just come on duty, gently shook his shoulder and tried to wake him up. "Sean? Come on Sean, you need to wake up." Seeing his eyelids flutter she went on, "That's right sweetheart, come on."

"Wh-what?" Sean's eyes abruptly snapped open as he struggled to come up from the depths of sleep. "Where am I? Oh God, where's Christi?"

"Shhh." the nurse cautioned quietly and in a gentle soothing way that all nurses seemed to have. "You were having a nightmare. Do you know why your here?"

"I, um, I was driving and this turn came up and I think I was going too fast and I, I, I, oh God!," Sean rambled covering his eyes with his hands, "where's Christi? Is Christi ok?"

The nurse, who at that moment was checking the array of machines that were surrounding Sean's bed said as if she hadn't heard him, "You have quite the bump on your head but other than that you seem to be fine. The doctor will be by in the morning to check on you and you will probably be released tomorrow. I'll send your parent's in here in just a moment."

Sean, who was feeling like it was time to take another nap, just sat there and stared at her, feeling as if he was still in a dream.

#

"Sean, its Mom. Are you awake honey?"

Sean heard his mothers sweet voice and tried to wake up. "Mum?" he mumbled.

"Yes baby, I'm here."

"Mum? Where's Christi?" Sean asked in a whisper, his eyes still closed. "Is she ok? Did she get hurt at all?"

His mom, now had tears streaming down her face but was doing her best to keep the sobs in so as not to frighten Sean was silent; afraid that speaking would be her undoing.

Sean finally opened his eyes and looked at his mom. Seeing the pain and sorrow in her eyes he knew. "No. Please. Tell me no. Mom. Please. Oh God. NOOO!!"

Sean couldn't hold it in any more. Somewhere deep inside he had known, but now it was reality. "Mom? Oh Mom. I'm so sorry."

She reached out and grabbed his hand, trying to placate him "Sean, sweetie, shhh. I know baby, it wasn't your fault. Christi in a good place, just remember that."

Sean, who couldn't stop the tears that were flowing from his eyes, just laid there in a thick silence. The only sounds you could hear was the uneven breathing of someone trying to control their sobs and the beep-beep of the nearby machines. Finally Sean said "Where's Dad?"

"Uh, Dad went home. He said he needed to be by himself right now." She replied hesitantly. "But he'll be here first thing in the morning." She was quick to add.

"You get some sleep now sweetie, I'll be right here."

And Sean slept and he dreamt. He dreamt that his dad was yelling at him,
blaming him for taking away his 'little girl.' He dreamt fitfully throughout the night and awoke the next morning to sunlight

filtering through the curtained windows, trying to make the drab room look more cheerful then it ever could be.

He saw his mother, with her short red hair mussed, and looking like she had aged ten years in twenty-four hours, laying sideways in a upright chair, sleeping, but without a peacefulness around her. Not wanting to disturb her, but badly needing to use the facilities he pushed the call button for a nurse. As one rushed in, not the one from the night before, he allowed her to help him out of bed and to the bathroom, but he stopped at allowing them to remain in the small room with him.

As he returned to his bed he saw that his mother was up and was just hanging up the phone that he had not heard ring. She was paler this morning and had tears in her eyes as she looked at her son.

"Is Dad coming?" Sean asked before she could speak.

"Oh Honey. Come sit down," she said with a pain filled voice as she patted the bed beside her.

Sean did as she asked and turned to her, "What is it Mom? What's the matter?"

"Your Dad, well he --"

She couldn't seem to look Sean in the eyes, "You see," she tried again, "Christi -- Christi was your father's baby. His little princess," Her eyes were starting to tear up again, Sean had a sinking feeling that whatever she was about to say, he didn't want to hear.

"Honey," she said taking his trembling hand in her own "your Dad couldn't handle it. Baby, last night he ...he ... he killed himself." and then she broke down, sobbing in great big gulps, trying to hold back, knowing that if she let go, it would be a long time before she ended.

Finally Sean, not able to stand his mother's pain any longer, knelt beside her and tried to mumble words of encouragement "Shh. Mom, we'll make it. You've got me. Shh. It's alright mom. It will be alright."

And Mother and son sat there like that for hours, just holding onto each other and the love that they had for their two lost loved ones.

Secret Family

My day started normal enough; the alarm woke me at 6:00am as usual, the coffee was as strong as normal, the kids got off to school with no mishaps and my email inbox was full of junk mail. Just a regular morning on a regular day.

Until the phone rang; shattering my quiet morning.

"Hello?" I answered with not a little irritation.

"I'm looking for Mrs. X," a gravelly voice replied.

"Uh, this is she, who is this?"

For a span of seconds all I heard was gargled breathing and then the man said, "Mrs. X, this is Mr. Smith at the Westwood Nursing Home, your presence is requested."

"Westwood?" I repeated, confused.

I didn't know anybody at Westwood, or any nursing home for that matter. "What is this about?"

"Ma'am, we'll explain everything to you when you arrive, how soon can you be here?"

"Wait! What? I don't know *anybody* at Westwood! What is this about??"

I heard the man sigh and say, "Is this or is this not Mrs. X?"

"Yes, I told you, it is."

"Then please come down, and we will explain everything." Having seemingly made himself clear, he hung up and I was left staring dumbfounded at my phone receiver, listening to the dial tone.

"Well." I mumbled to myself as I dialed my husband's office number. "Honey," I started to explain when he was on the line, "I just received the weirdest phone call!"

He waited until I had finished replaying the phone call for him and replied, "What could it hurt? Head down there and just see what they want. You never know, maybe your long lost Aunt left you a bundle of money and I can quit working!"

His laugh rumbled over the line and I couldn't help smiling as I heard it. I knew I didn't have a long lost Aunt, but he was right, what could it hurt? I really had nothing better to do.

As I walked through the door of Westwood Nursing Home, the first thing I noticed was How worn down everything was. *Not a place I'd put my mother*, I thought to myself.

The brown carpet was faded and worn with stains that I was better off not knowing about; the furniture mismatched and scattered around. I approached the front desk, little more than a folding table with a computer, phone and printer on it.

"Um, my name is Mrs. X, Mr. Smith called me earlier and asked me to stop by?"

The white haired lady smiled a toothless grin and reached for the phone. "Mr. Smith, Mrs. X has arrived."

She looked up at me and told me to have a seat, he'd be right out.

I looked around at the dingy furniture and decided that standing would be my best bet.

A small man with graying hair and a gauntly limp came out of a side hallway and walked towards me, hand out stretched. "Mrs. X, thank you for coming," he said as he shook my hand. "Please follow me."

I followed behind him, peeking into windows where I could. I saw what I presumed was a game room; men and woman playing cards, chess and monopoly on small card tables. I saw one woman working a puzzle that took up an entire table, the edges hanging off the table.

One room we passed held a bunch of run down picnic tables, which I guessed was the dining room. A few doors down from the dining room Mr. Smith opened a windowless door and gestured for me to go first.

The first thing to hit me as I walked in the small, dim room was the stench. It smelled like menthol and disinfectant, in that order.

I sat in the metal folding chair across from the first real piece of furniture I had seen sense arriving. Mr. Smith's desk was massive, all wood, polished and gleaming. Obviously the man had made his office his domain.

He had a manila folder sitting squarely in the middle of his desk and as he sat, he opened it.

"Mrs. X", he began, "does the name John Bishop mean anything to you?"

I shook my head no as I told him, "I don't know any Bishop's."

Mr. Smith slid a photograph out of the folder and pushed it across the desk to me. "This is John." He explained, "he was a resident here for a little over eight years. He passed away in his sleep last Sunday"

"Oh!" I didn't know what to say. I didn't know this John man and I still didn't know why I was here.

"John was a wealthy man, he could have gone to a much nicer facility, but he chose to live here for reasons he never shared."

"Mrs. X, John's will states that his estate is to go to his great niece, Sandra Lynn X, which is you."

"Wait. What?" I was extremely confused; I didn't know any Bishops and a great uncle? Where did he come from?

"My maiden name is Bruchard; my mother's maiden name is Perry, I can't see how I am related to this man."

Mr. Smith pulled out some more documents and explained, "Apparently Bishop is the American name for Bruchard. John was your grandfather's estranged brother and he chose to Americanize his name. His estate is worth a little over five million dollars and he left it all to you along with this." He handed her an envelope, sealed, with her name scrawled across the front. "Our lawyers are drawing up the documents and they should be ready by the end of the week for you to sign. Any questions?"

"Uh, no. No. I'm just - - I'm a little shocked. I didn't know my grandfather had any siblings, they were never mentioned. This is - - this is - - wow!"

Mr. Smith stood up and shook my hand, "I'll be in touch Mrs. X and good luck to you."

I walked myself out through the dingy hallways, my mind racing thousands of miles a minute. When I reached my car I slipped a nail under the flap of the envelope and extracted a single piece of paper. I read through the scrawled handwriting once, and then stopped and reread it again.

To my niece,

I am sorry that we never had a chance to get to know one another. You are my only living relative and I pray that what little I am able to leave you is sufficient. Enjoy your adult life; it goes quickly.

Yours truly,

Great Uncle John

I pulled out my phone and punched in my husband's office number.

"Hey honey," I said when he came on the line, "Well, sad to say, it wasn't a great Aunt with bundles of money."

My husband laughed and replied, "Ahh well. Another day, another dollar. Guess I won't quit my job after all."

"Well, perhaps. But there was a great uncle," I told him as I started to laugh as I hugged the letter to my chest.

It's Who I Am

There was no easy way to say goodbye, that was for sure, but Rob always held out hope that maybe it wouldn't hurt as bad the next time.

Unfortunately, it just seemed to hurt worse, and he wasn't sure how many more times he could do this before he finally crumbled. The hole in his heart that had been present since childhood only grew bigger each time someone passed through his life; someone whom he'd thought would finally make him become the man he wanted to be.

But he was still the little boy he'd always hated; and he desperately wanted to grow up.

"Cadie, I'm sorry! I really didn't mean to –

"To sleep with another woman the very same night that I flew in to see you? God damn you, Rob - what the hell were you thinking? Wasn't I enough for you?"

"Of course you were, Cades. It's not you that has the problem, it's me." He sighed laboriously and sat down on the edge of the creaking hotel bed, looking up at his girlfriend with blue eyes outlined in an alcoholic pink. "It's always me."

Cadie Vega began to shove her things back into her suitcase as quickly as she had emptied it only hours ago. Her long, dark hair was coming loose from the drooping bun she had swept it up in, and her green eyes were blazing with fury. "I'm tired of playing the role of understanding, dismissing girlfriend to your pathetic, screwed-up delusion of a musician! And I'm so fucking tired of pretending to be blind to every woman you flirt with and every goddamned affair that you think I don't know about!"

She stopped what she was doing and straightened, staring at the wall for several long seconds before turning to face him. "You know, I thought it would be different for us - I thought that maybe I would be the woman who finally loved you well enough to make you change."

"You did love me well, Cades," Rob promised her, blinking away the abrupt onset of tears that he didn't want her to see. "God, honey - you loved me more then I deserved."

"But it still wasn't enough, I guess." Her voice was a whisper, and she turned back to her suitcase, pulling the top flap closed without bothering to fold the contents inside. Stepping back, she reached for the leather purse that she had set down on the nightstand beside the large bed, and slid it onto her shoulder. "My sister lives about twenty minutes from here, so I think I'll make the most of this trip and go see her. Will you send my bag over to the Radisson on Dock Avenue? I'm gonna rent a car after I get to her house."

"You don't have to go," Rob told her. "Please don't go Cadie. Stay, we can work through this." His voice shook as he spoke the words, but he knew that they were empty and worthless. He'd done irreparable damage to whatever it was that he'd once had with this woman, and no amount of emotional pleading would keep her from walking through the door and away from what he had done to her.

Cadie kneeled down and took his trembling hand from where it lay on his lap, bringing it to her lips, and kissing it lovingly.

He felt an unseen tear splash onto his palm from her closing eyes, and he inhaled sharply, afraid that if he didn't he would soon forget to breathe.

"As much as I want to hate you right now, Rob, I can't. I could never do anything but adore you. You do that to people, you know. You make women fall at your feet with just one glance of those sad, blue eyes."

Her lids fluttered open, and she focused on his beautiful face, its lines so imperfectly wonderful that she knew her eyes would miss it almost as much as her heart. "But I can't stay here. I know that you didn't want to hurt me - you never want to hurt anyone - but the fact is, you're not as emotionally invested in this relationship as I am, and without that reciprocation there's nothing here for me."

"I'm sorry," he said on a wobbly sigh. "I wanted this to work. I wanted you to be the last beautiful girl that I loved."

"Me too," she whispered. "Only problem is, you don't love me as I love you." She abruptly released his hand, as if it had suddenly grown scalding, and absently reached up to fold a lock of raven hair behind her ear. "I'm gonna go back to your place in a few days and get my things, give notice at work, and then I'll probably head home to Memphis." She straightened up and adjusted the bag on her shoulder as Rob got to his feet. "My mom will be happy to see me, and I think I can get my old job back."

"The library?"

Cadie smiled wanly and nodded. "Yeah, back to the Dewey decimal system and wiping grape jam fingerprints off the pages of Harry Potter books." She shrugged half-heartedly, and cut her eyes away. "It won't be so bad. Maybe I'll even go back to school, finish my psyche degree. In a few years, you can pay me to put up with your shit."

His face paled and she reached out to touch his arm. "I'm sorry. I didn't mean to be that way. I guess I just haven't perfected my act yet - it's not every day that you have to walk out on the only man you've ever loved."

"Cades..." He reached for her but she pulled away.
"I should go - no sense in dragging this out. Besides," she said, shrugging lightly, her eyes flooding as he looked on, helpless. "I guess I always knew it would end like this, and I always knew we'd both be crying for different reasons."

"Saying I'm sorry again seems so stupid, but I don't know what else to offer you."

"What else is there?"

Rob glanced at the clock on the nightstand surface. In two hours he would have to face the other guys at sound check and scramble to find yet another explanation as to why his latest relationship hadn't worked out. And they had all really liked Cadie; after he'd divorced Marisa, his friends and family would have gratefully accepted almost anyone

"Your room will be reserved by the time you get to the Radisson," he told her, aware that they had exhausted everything else there was. "Will you let me get someone to drive you over to your sister's?"

She shook her head. "Cab fare will be fine." He nodded wordlessly, and slid a hand into his pants pocket to search for the fifty-dollar bill he'd shoved in there after paying for dinner earlier. It was crumpled up in a ball, and he retrieved it, smoothing it out before handing it to her. The gesture seemed almost symbolic, as if removing the wrinkles would dull the blunt edge of the end. "Is that enough?"

She stared at the bill for a few long seconds, and then her face rose to meet his. "It'll get me to my sister's place, if that's what you mean." He tried to speak but she cut him off. "Be careful with my bags, there are some breakable things in there. Oh, and the smaller one has some traveler's checks in the front pocket so make sure that it's tightly zipped before you ship it to the hotel." Her voice drifted off and her shoulders rose and fell. "Take care of yourself, Rob. You're pretty easy to keep tabs on, ya know - what with being famous and all."

He allowed a modest smile. "Yeah, that."

She nodded one last time and then turned towards the door. As she drew it open, and began to step out of the room, she turned back to have a final look at the man that she had always known would break her heart. "See ya around. Be good."

He nodded because he couldn't speak, and watched as she closed the door; the thud echoing its finality.

Waiting on Flight 7768

The airport waiting room crackled with the frustration of 94 passengers peeved at the seeming endless delays their flight was encountering. I sat staring out the window at the planes on the tarmac, where they had been for the last five hours, unmoving.

The woman next to me turned her head towards me and started talking as if we were long lost friends.

"They can delay the flight as much as they want; this will still be better than my last trip to Atlanta. Oh, I tell you—I'll *never* forget that trip. It was Labor Day weekend, see? And my husband, well he was my fiancé then, was taking me and the kids to meet his folks in Atlanta. I guess I should tell you that I had four kids from my first marriage, and his family hadn't met any of us. So naturally, I was a little nervous as you might expect. But the weekend turned out really nice and we all got along real good."

I nodded, wondering if I had talk to me stamped on my forehead.

"Well, the highlight of the weekend was that Saturday night when we went to one of those Japanese steak house places. You know, the kind where they cook it right there at the table and they throw the knives around and all that? It was his mom's birthday, my husband's mom that is, and my oldest son's birthday was just a couple of days before, so we made it a big family thing. Anyway, his sister talked us all into trying some sushi, something called a California roll. And it wasn't half-bad. I mean, I don't know if I could eat a whole meal of that, but at least I can say I've tried it. I can't say for sure, but I think that's where our problems started.

"We get up Sunday morning and piled everybody in the mini-van to start out early because it's like a 12-hour drive from Atlanta. We hadn't been on the road for an hour when my little 3-year-old tells me she's about to throw up! Well, we headed for the side of the road quick as we could, but just not quite quick enough. The poor little things got spit up down the front of her shirt and all in her lap and she's crying her eyes out. We got her out of van and tried to clean her up best we could—it was still dark, you know. We took off her clothes and dug out some new ones from her suitcase. I just never WILL forget the sight of that little girl standing in her panties on the side of the expressway with the light of those passing 18-wheelers shining on her!" Here she laughs, as if she has just said the funniest thing on earth. I scan the flight monitor, trying not to be rude, but trying to get the message across that I am not interested in her story. She didn't get the message.

"Of course, I'm just thinking she's a little carsick. We stopped at the next exit and got her some Sprite to settle her stomach. But as the day went on, none of us felt real good. We thought we were just tired, what with all the excitement and the long hours in the van. We even managed to eat a pretty good dinner at the Western Sizzlin' somewhere in Alabama. But then just about sunset, Donnie—that's my oldest—he says he's feeling a little sick. Well, you have to understand that Donnie was a little bit of a hypochondriac back then. You know, thought he was allergic to everything if it would get him a little attention."

"We figured he was trying his old trick of claiming to get carsick if he didn't sit up front with the driver. Right up until he yelled 'Quick, pull over!' You guessed it, all over the middle bench seat of the van. As luck would have it, we had just passed the entrance to a rest area not seconds before his warning so there was nowhere to go but the emergency lane."

Here she stops and takes a sip of her coffee. I think that now would be a good time to go for a walk, but before I can start to stand she starts again.

"Poor Donnie, he jumped out of the van and spilled his guts, so to speak, on the side of the road. My poor fiancé; I saw him jump out of the driver's seat and rush around to our side of the van. I was touched at his concern for his soon-to-be stepson until I realized that he was getting out to barf himself. Seems the smell of vomit inside that van was too much for him and he joined Donnie in his roadside purge. Once again, we tried to clean up everyone and everything as best we could. We stopped at the next exit for Lysol and wash towels, though I'm not sure the smell of all that disinfectant wasn't nearly as bad.

"By this time, we're only about 2 hours or so away from home and we're just praying to make it there without further disaster. But you know how the smell of vomit is, kind of triggers the same reaction in you when you smell it? Well, I don't know if it was that, or he just decided it was his turn, but my son Mark—the quiet one—says 'Momma, I think I'm gonna throw up.' Now you have to know that he says this right as we were driving through what you would call *not the best part of town,*" this last part she whispers and I turn to look at her, expecting to see a group of thugs standing near her; I see nothing to note why she would start whispering and think again that now would be a good time to go for a walk.

She starts talking again in a normal voice, "So we ask him, 'how sure are you,' because finding a safe place to pull over might not be the easiest thing around here. First he says he thinks he'll be okay, but then a few minutes later- just in time to get into an even worse part of town—he says he really thinks he's gonna puke. Well, my fiancé hit the next exit, searching desperately for a well-lit service station. He's heading down one street and up another, I swear he was rounding corners on two-wheels. But not finding any place that he felt was safe enough. Meanwhile, poor Mark is just clenching his jaw and turning so pale he was practically glowing in the dark. Finally, he can hold it no longer and he re-christens the back of the van. That was enough for my fiancé: He pulled into the first place he could—right into the entrance to City Park. He barely had the car in Park before we all tumbled out and started retching in the darkness."

"It took us about ten minutes before we could regain any sense of composure and start thinking about cleaning out the van. Clothes were changed immediately, and we pulled out everything we could that had been touched by the vomit. I was in favor of just leaving everything there in the grass; there was no way I was going to put any of that smelly stuff back in the car. But fiancé was adamant we weren't going to just leave that stuff—clothes, floor mats, pillows—behind. He dug around in the back of the van and came out with a big plastic garbage bag that we had put all our dirty clothes in before leaving Atlanta. He dumped out the laundry, which by now was the best smelling thing in that van, and started gathering up the soiled items. I still was not going to be subjected to that smell, so he tied the bag to the roof rack by the yellow plastic handles, and after some more scrubbing and the rest of the can of Lysol, we were back on our way.

"Now, to give him the benefit of the doubt, he was tired and ill, and I'm sure if he hadn't been he would have known better. But we weren't back on the interstate a mile when that bag blew right off the roof and all over the freeway. But my beloved would not be beaten. Would you believe we looped back at the next exit and pulled up to where the bag flew off, and that man started running out getting each item one by one? You talk about a sight! The kids and I sitting in the van about a quarter-mile back so we could see traffic coming around the curve, blowing the horn each time a car approached, then cheering and blinking the headlights every time he retrieved something. If our stomachs hadn't already been hurting, they would have been then from laughing so hard."

"He finally gathered all of our stuff up and even the plastic bag, which we placed squarely between my knees in the front seat. We rocketed home at 80 miles an hour with every window open in the chilly night air, trying to outrun the smell inside the van. As we turned into my driveway, he looked at me and said, 'Sorry. Nice try, but it didn't work.' Of course, I didn't know what he was talking about, so he continued, 'Nice try at scaring me off, but I still want to marry you. If we can survive this day, the rest should be a breeze.' "

She giggles, and again I turn to look at her. This time I feel like I should say something. "That' quite a story," I say, "I'm glad it all worked out."

BEEP - *Flight 7768 to Atlanta is now boarding, all passengers please proceed to gate 8.* The overhead speaker system repeated itself.

"Well," I said as I gathered my carryon and headed to the gate, "It was nice meeting you, and best of luck."

It Wasn't Murder

"It wasn't murder," said Tom Dotson

The words rang false in the small windowless interrogation room.

It was murder most foul. Detective Jennings knew it was murder.

The massive head wound and the burial place of the body eliminated any chance of an accidental death.

With a groan of disapproval, Detective Jennings turned off the tape recorder. He pushed his face so close to Tom's before speaking, that it looked like he was going to bite him. His stale coffee breath covered Tom's face.

"Listen son," the grizzled old detective said between clenched teeth, "When you waived your right to an attorney and agreed to talk, I expected you to tell the truth."

"But it is the truth," protested Tom.

The huge detective pushed himself away from the table waving his hand in a sweeping arc like a traffic cop to cut off

Tom's objections. He pointed to the tape recorder with his index finger.

"In a minute, I'm going to turn the recorder back on, and I want you to answer my questions truthfully. Telling lies will just get you deeper into trouble. Do you understand what I am saying to you???"

"Yes, sir."

Tom Dotson was just a baby-faced kid. He was a sophomore at Bradley High School. He looked too young to be involved in murder. He looked too innocent.

Detective Jenning's figured he weighed three times as much as this baby-faced killer. His own face was weather beaten and wrinkled. His ex-wife claimed he looked like a walrus with a mustache. For him, murder was no longer a mystery.

He was a jaded police detective who had seen and heard it all.

When Detective Jennings switched the tape recorder back on, he stood up. It was a classic ploy of intimidation. He towered over the boy. He would scare the truth out of him if nothing else worked.

"OK, for the record it is Saturday November 2nd, at aah 2:45 p.m., and I am interviewing Tom Dotson who has come to the Westminster Police Station to make a statement concerning the murder of Lori Bennett. He has agreed to waive his right to silence and right to an attorney and understands his Miranda Warning. Is that correct Mr. Dotson?"

"Yes, it is."

"OK. Were you a friend of the deceased, Lori Bennett?"

"Yes, we were both sophomores at Bradley High School."

"Did you take Miss Bennett to the Deerfield Cemetery on the night of her death?"

"Yes."

"Did you plan ahead what you were going to do that night?"

Tom Dotson squirmed in his chair. He pulled at the back of his hair with his right hand. His lower lip quivered as if he were going to confess, but he swallowed the words. "Yes, I . . . aah, well . . . aah, we sorta planned it together."

"Together?"

"Yeah," said Tom trying to look innocent.

The detective started walking around Tom's chair. He made a complete circuit before asking his next question. When he stopped, he was standing directly behind the chair that Tom sat in.

"But you came up with the idea first, didn't you?"

"Yeah."

Standing behind the suspect, Detective Jennings allowed himself a sad, knowing smirk. This was going to be easy. He was an expert at interrogation. Everything was planned. If it was pre-meditation, he could shoot for Murder I. His next round of questions would focus on motivation. The noose was tightening.

He grabbed the other chair and sat down next to the suspect. He lowered his voice. In a good imitation of a funeral director, with his eyes downcast, he continued the questioning in a confidential, sympathetic voice.

"You loved her didn't you?"

Tom shifted uncomfortably on the hard chair. He opened his mouth and closed it without saying anything. He swallowed hard and bit his lower lip. He looked down at his tennis shoes and lifted his head until his eyes locked with the detective's.

"Yes, I loved her."

"Was she your girlfriend?"

"Yes. No. She was Max Birmingham's girlfriend."

"Why did you say 'Yes'?"

"Well, she used to be my girlfriend. She was my true love. She still is my true love," Tom said, his eyes drifting to the table and his lips quavering.

Hiding his expression of disgust, Detective Jennings rubbed his right hand over his forehead. He already knew the ending. Murder. Now he knew the beginning. True Love. He had to ask the remaining questions just to wrap things up. Just for the record. Pointing an accusatory finger at Tom, he got right to the crux of the problem.

"You loved her, but Max Birmingham loved her too, didn't he?."

"No! I loved Lori. Max didn't love her! He used her!"

"Why would she think that?"

"Max was a player, a smooth-talking kind of guy. He told Lori whatever he thought she wanted to hear."

"Like what?"

"He'd tell her she was beautiful. He'd say he loved her. He was fast. He didn't waste time."

"So Lori fell for this Birmingham guy?"

"Yeah, he was a phony. I tried to warn Lori, but she just blew me off as being jealous."

Detective Jennings leaned back in his chair. There it was.

Jealousy.

He knew it. Maybe he should try to shorten the Q & A. Maybe he should go right for the kill. In a tired, but understanding voice like a parent who already knew his kid had broken the rules, he flung out the key question with feigned indifference.

"You loved Lori so much you couldn't share her with Birmingham so you killed her. Didn't you?"

"No!"

"Well, she's dead, isn't she?"

"Yes, she's dead."

"And you're responsible."

"Yes." Tom sighed, a defeated look on his face. "Yes, I'm responsible."

Detective Jennings was getting closer. Tom admitted being responsible. The killing blow to Lori's skull by a shovel had been deliberate. If he was responsible, he was the killer.

It was time to turn up the pressure.

With no warning, the detective slammed his open hand down on the table top with a thunderous clap.

"Bull Shit!" the detective shouted.

Tom cowered at the sudden outburst. His eyes darted around in alarm looking for a way out. There was no escape. The kid could not run away so he tried talking his way out. He would say anything to avoid the wrath of the huge detective.

"Cut the crap!" shouted the detective.

"I was going to marry Lori!" Tom Dotson shouted back. "It was true love. No one loved Lori more than I did. She even wrote the letters T.L.N.D. on the fingers of her left hand. They stood for 'True Love Never Dies'. We were going to get married until Max Birmingham came along. Max conned Lori. He won her heart with lies."

The detective interrupted him.

"How did you know they were lies?"

"Because of the prank."

"What prank?"

"You know; the cemetery."

"Tell me about it."

Detective Jennings made a mental note to check the autopsy report for any mention of inked initials on the victim's fingers.

Tom continued his confession.

"We decided to play a practical joke on Max. But it was a joke with a purpose. It would prove to Lori that his love for her was false. Me and a couple of other guys - -"

"Which guys?" the detective interrupted.

"Just some school friends."

"What were their names?"

"James Russell and Bret Daniels."

"OK. So you and these guys take Max to the cemetery," said the detective to get things back on track.

"Yeah, we take Max out at night to this freshly dug open grave. It had mounds of dirt around it. The shovels were still in the hole along with a casket."

"Where did the casket come from?"

"We stole it from the Haunted House for the Bradley High School Halloween Party. We were going to return it. We told Max that Lori had been killed in a car accident. It was dark. We pointed our flashlights at the casket. We dared him to open the lid. He bragged that he was a pragmatist. He said dead bodies did not bother him. Lori was laying inside the casket with white powder covering her face and hands. When Max lifted the lid, Lori fluttered her eyelids and started reaching for him."

Tom stopped talking.

"So what happened?"

"I don't know. We all screamed, pretending to be scared, and ran out of the cemetery."

"So you left Max and Lori alone together?"

"That's right."

"What did you do next?"

"We waited."

"How long?"

"For about an hour."

"What happened?"

"Nothing."

"Nothing?"

"Neither Max nor Lori left the cemetery. I wanted to find out why, but the other guys held me back. They said to leave the Love birds alone. They said Lori was getting it on with Max in the casket. The joke had backfired. So we went home."

The detective urged Tom to continue with a circular wave of his hand.

"The next day at school, we expected Max to be mad, but instead he was ice cold. I was the hot one. When we started razzing him about how 'True Love Never Dies', Max surprised us all. He got angry. He said we were a bunch of ghouls. He said we were sickos and necrophilia's. He had a deadly serious look on his face.

"Well, we may be necrophilia's," I challenged him, "but where is Lori?"

"You know where Lori is," Max answered, and he walked away.

Detective Jennings looked at Tom Dotson with genuine interest. Maybe this was not murder. Maybe it was something else. A disturbing series of images started forming in his mind.

"Did you see it happen?"

"I never saw it, but I can't get it out of my mind."

Tom Dobson went on to describe exactly what Detective Jennings was thinking. It was as if Dobson were reading his mind.

Lori was reaching up to grab Max, pulling him toward her for a kiss, saying true love never dies. Max must have been in a panic. He was trapped in a grave with the living dead. Flailing his hands to escape, he must have dropped the flashlight. In his blind groping, he found the shovel hand. He hit her over the head. Then to stop her from coming after him, he did the practical thing. He buried her.

Despite the story having the ring of truth to it, Detective Jennings gave Tom Dobson a puzzled look.

"How can you be so sure it wasn't murder?"

"Because Max was deadly serious. He never got the joke."

"How was he supposed to know it was a joke?"

"Don't you know?"

"Humor me."

"It happened on October 31st."

"So?"

"It was Halloween."

A Bear Saves The Day

It was evening in the forest, gray mist was rising from the gray and green wet moss, water was trickling down from the gray clouds. The sand road that went through it, lined with tall dark green birch trees, was full of mud pools. The only signs of use on the road were a few empty beer cans on the side of the road.

From the distance you could hear the sound of a whining car engine, growing louder by the second, until a blue mud covered Jeep with four muddy lights appeared, racing from mud pool to mud pool.

Behind the windshield you could just make out the figures of two laughing men. Just as the men thought they had made a clean getaway they drove into a mud pool that was a little bit deeper than they had expected. The whole front end of the jeep sank. Smoke rising from the engine, the engine sputtered and then died.

" DAMN IT!," the black haired middle aged man wearing camouflage in the driver's seat shouted, slamming his hands on the steering wheel in frustration.

"Take it easy John," the man sitting next to him, with cropped hair, jeans and a black leather jacket said to him as he opened the door. The muddy water rushed in to the Jeep through the open door. "Fuck!" he swore.

"But you said to take it easy Bob," John said to him, with a smile.

"Shut up, Bob growled.

Both John and Bob got out of the Jeep, their pants wet from the muddy water. Gray mist rose from their mouths with each breath they took.

John started to chuckle.

"Stop laughing man, not none of this shit is funny!" Bob said.

John laughed even harder, bending at the waste.

"What the hell are you laughing at?" Bob yelled at John.

"Look at us man! Here we are, with thousands of dollars in grocery sacks, soaking wet, freezing and I the middle of nowhere!"

"Shit!! The money!'" Bob remembered, sprinting to the back of the Jeep. He opened the backdoors and there sat two white grocery sacks. "The money is all right," he breathed as John walked to his side.

"Gimme five man," Bob offered his black glove for John. John slammed it, hard, laughing once again.

"Hey man, cheer up! Consider it this way; if we can walk out of here, we're golden!" John said.

"Yeah and we sure as hell have got a lot of walking to do, so let's move it," Bob said, shaking his head with a hint of smile.

John and Bob walked in the twilight, with the white bags tied to ends of branches, going over their shoulders, both hands holding them from the front end.

"You should have seen that cashier when I drew the gun; he sure peed in his pants for sure!" Bob exclaimed, breathing heavily.

"Hey, look at that," John said, pointing at a dark figure standing at the middle of the road about hundred and fifty meters away from them.

They both stopped.

The figure was moving towards them, and it looked huge. Both John and Bob dropped the bags and reached for their guns in their side holsters. As the figure came closer, they could hear a weird grunting sound.

"Shit!" Bob cried, "It's a bear!"

Both men turned to run the way they had come. "Damn! John, quick, grab the money!"

John quickly turned back around and took two fast steps to where the money lay, grabbing the bags, he raced back to Bob.

"Shit, what're we gonna do Bob?" John asked, stopping to look behind him. The bear was stilling coming towards them, but he seemed to not be in any particular hurry. John watched as the bear stopped and pawed the ground for a moment before continuing on.

"Well we can't go back," Bob said. "The cops are gonna be on our trail real soon, if they aren't already. We've both got guns and know how to use em'." Bob smiled, showing his teeth, and continued, "Let's go kill us a bear."

"Shhh! I think I heard something!" John exclaimed, cocking his head in the direction that they had left their Jeep.

Very faintly, the men could hear sirens coming their way. "That doesn't sound like just one cop to me," John observed.

"Shit." Bob cursed. "It just went from bad to worse."

He glanced between the way they had come and the bear for a moment. "Ok," he said, coming to a conclusion in his mind. "The cops sound like they are still a ways back. Plus, they aren't gonna be able to get around our Jeep. They're gonna have to come in on foot, just like we did."

"We have to get around that bear and run like hell. That's the only way out of this that I see."

"You sure these little pistols can take down a big bear like that?" wondered John. "Because I kinda like having my arms and legs."

"It may not stop him, but it sure will slow him down," Bob answered as he checked his gun, making sure it was ready to fire. "On three. Ready?"

"As ready as I can be, I guess," John replied, removing his gloves and wiping his hands down the side of his jeans. He took a deep breath and brought his gun to position.

"One. Two. Three!!" Bob yelled, running forward with his gun straight out in front of him. John followed close behind him and to the right. Bob's first shot missed his target and John took aim. As he shot, the bear charged forward, coming after the men.

"Shoot him! Damn it! Shoot! Shoot!" cried John.

"Forget it John! Just run!" Bob shouted, running back down the road towards the stuck Jeep.

John turned and followed Bob, shooting behind him every fifteen feet at the bear. But the bear showed no fear towards the bullets. If anything, it seemed to anger him more.

"Shit! Bob, what're we gonna do?" John shouted, breathless. Bob was about ten feet in front of him, glancing back every once in a while to make sure the bear wasn't closing in.

They came to the Jeep, mud glistening in the moonlight. Lights sprang on all around them, "FREEZE!" someone yelled. "Hands in the air!" Drop the gun! I SAID DROP THE GUN!!"

John and Bob complied with the instructions, dropping their guns into the mud pit and raising their hands high over their heads.

"A bear!" Bob started, "There's a bear!"

"Shut up!" an officer screamed just as they heard a roar. Everybody turned to look, and there stood the bear on his two hind legs. He stretched towards the sky, an easy six feet tall.

BOOM

The bear fell with a muted thud.

Bob swiveled his head to look at the officers. One old grizzly of a man held a shotgun and said with a toothless grin "Well boys, I sure hated to kill that bear seeing as he had a hand in catching you creeps. But I'd rather kill him then allow that bear to kill you two. You deserve what's a coming to you."

"Ah shit Bob, we've been busted cuz' of a dumb bear," John sighed.

Made in the USA
Charleston, SC
30 December 2009